This book belongs to:

_____

Let's Talk!

Hello! My name is Uni, and I'm a unicorn.
Are you ready to take an adventure with me?

That's me and my mom in the picture.
She's really sweet, and I was a baby then.

I'm so excited to meet you! I love making new friends.
You can tell me about yourself when we get to that page.

I am ready to help you complete mazes,
color, read, and write a little.

Come on! Let's get going!!!

Let's Write, Color, and Draw!

You're going to need your pencil and crayons!

I want you to write about yourself
on the next page, and then,
you'll get to trace my name and color my picture!

 # ALL ABOUT ME

This is a picture of me

My name is
_____
_____
_____

When I grow up, I want to be a/an
_____
_____
_____
_____
_____

 I am _____ years old.

This year, I want to learn more about

1 _____
_____

2 _____
_____

3 _____
_____

Uni, the unicorn

Draw a picture of you and someone special. It can be your mom, dad, grandmother, or friend.
Then, write your name on the lines below.

It's Maze Time!

You're going to need your pencil and crayons!

Start

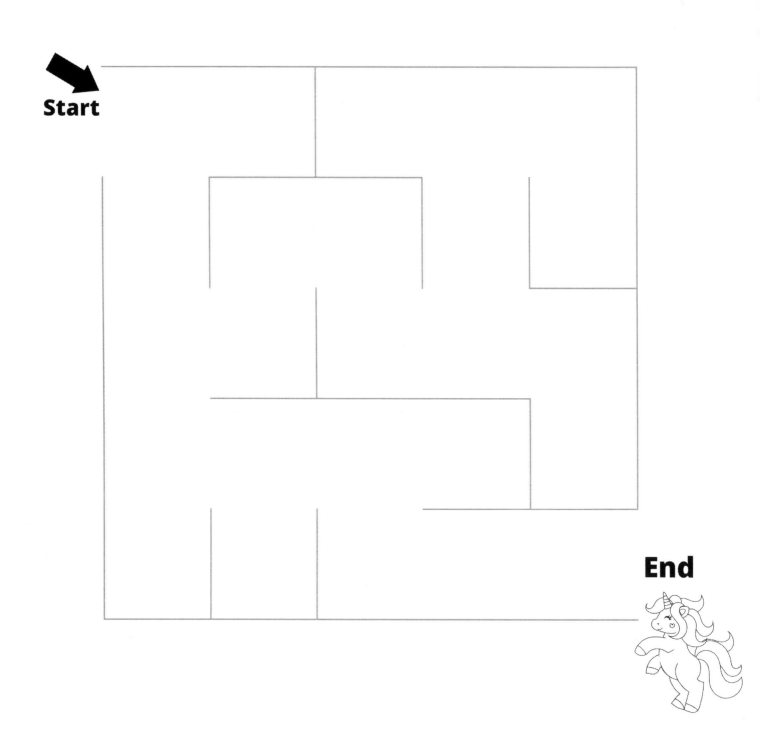

End

How did you do?
The answer is on the next page.

Start

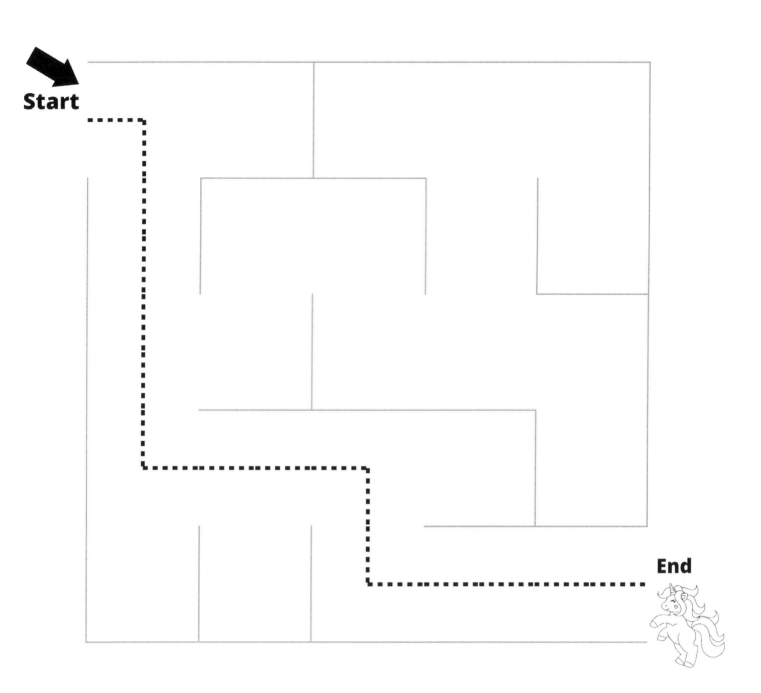

End

Great job! I knew you could do it! Some of the mazes may get a little harder later but don't worry, I'll be here to help you!

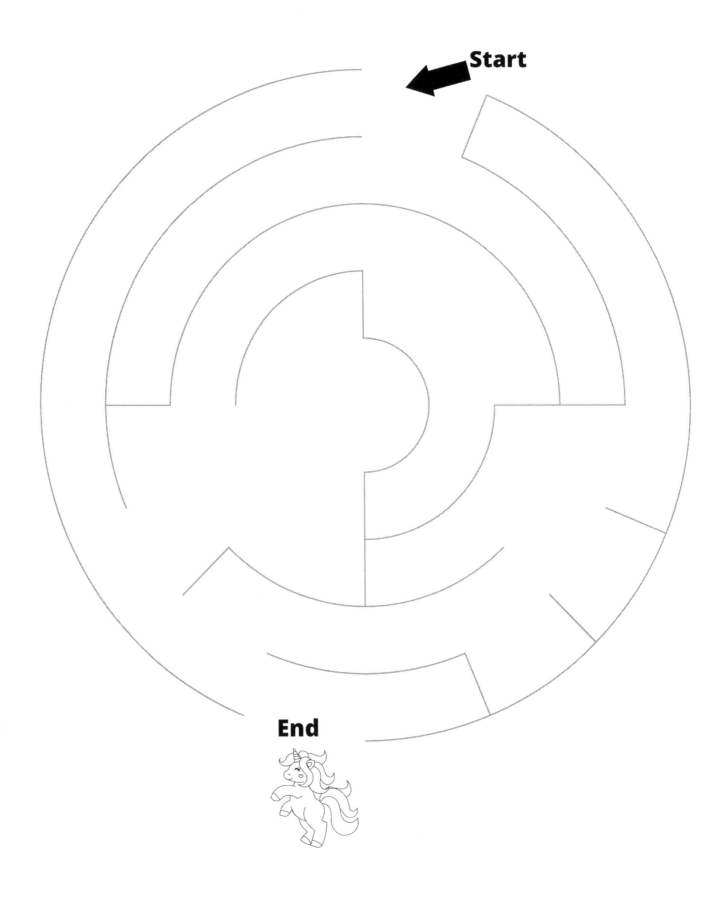

Start

End

Let's check out the answer on the next page.

Start

End

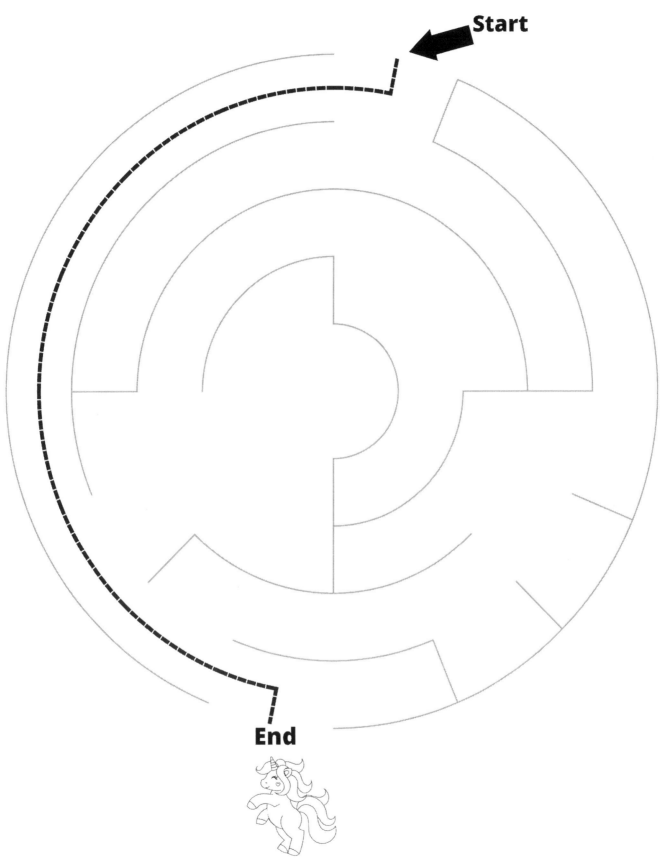

Amazing again! You are really good at this!

This one's a little bit harder, but I believe in you! See if you can find your way out!
No worries, the answer is on the next page.

Start

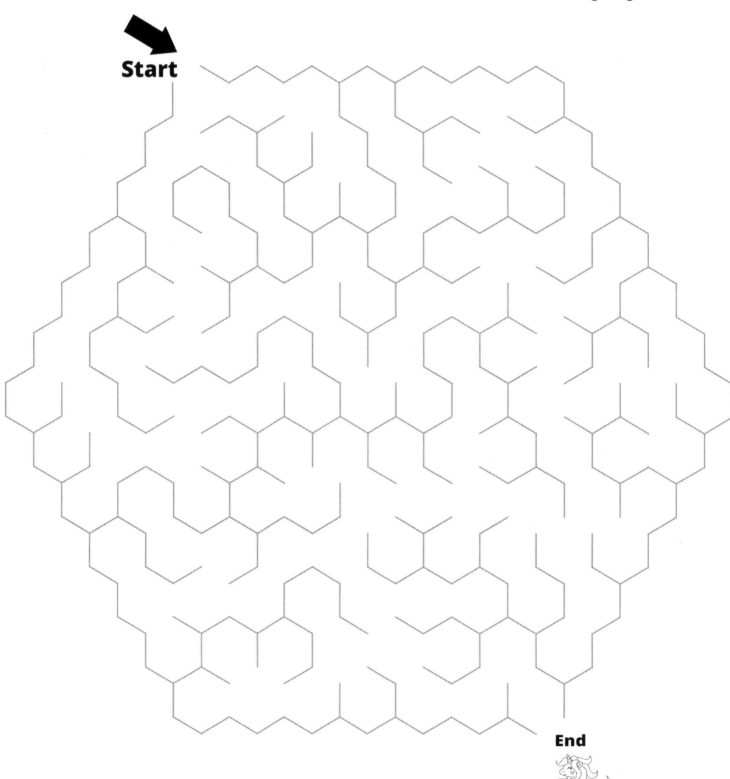

End

Winner! Winner!
You are really good at finding your way!

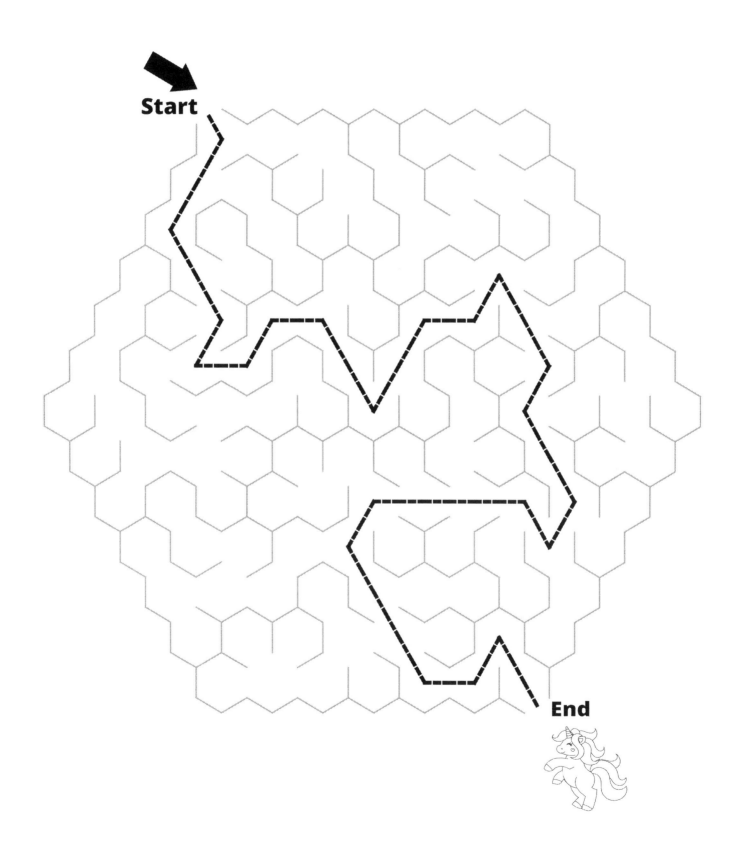

Start

End

Let's Read!

When I was born, I was very, very small. All of my friends grew quickly, and their horns—actually called an alicorn—grew big and long too. Mine was just a nub. You could barely see it. It looked like a little chicken nugget.

I was pretty sad.

Some of the other unicorns would laugh at me, and it made me extremely sad.

The size of my horn did not matter to my mother! She loved me and always encouraged me. Mom told me to be happy.

She also said a "**_real friend_**" would like me even if my horn was small. Then, she said exactly what I wanted to hear, "Uni, you are special, and one day your horn will grow! When it does, it will be amazing." I was so happy to hear that, and I believed it would grow, but it seemed to take forever.

My mom tried to help me feel better. She always found new ways to make me smile.

We went to the beach.

She let me play in the ball pit.

She let me play video games.

Sometimes, I just laid on the grass and talked to my friend "Butter". He was a really cool butterfly.

I would eat ice cream!
That is one of my faves.

I roller-skated, and I wasn't very good, but I didn't give up.

It was really kind of scary to see everyone flying around me on the skates. Some people moved so fast, but I had fun going slowly and trying to go faster.
I like roller skating, and think I'll skate really fast one day.

Eventually, I started making more friends—not all of them were unicorns. Tony was a kid like you. He loved to read, so we would read books together. He's super smart and wants to become a scientist one day.

I played in my treehouse a lot!
It was fun.

When I went to sleep, I dreamed I was flying in a rocket!

Even though I did a lot of fun things, I still wanted my horn to grow, but I knew it would take time.

My mom taught me a new word. She said, "Uni, you must be **patient**." That means sometimes you just have to wait.

I always tried to obey my mom.
She told me if I ate healthy food,
I would grow big and strong
and so would my horn.

And just like my mom said,
my horn started growing!
I was happy!

One day, I woke up and
this is what I saw! I
couldn't believe my eyes!

I was beautiful and strong! I also knew how to be a great friend. I never want to make anyone feel sad like I did. I know everyone is special. You are very special too, and I'm so glad we're friends!

Let's Color!

You'll get to color pictures of me and my friends.

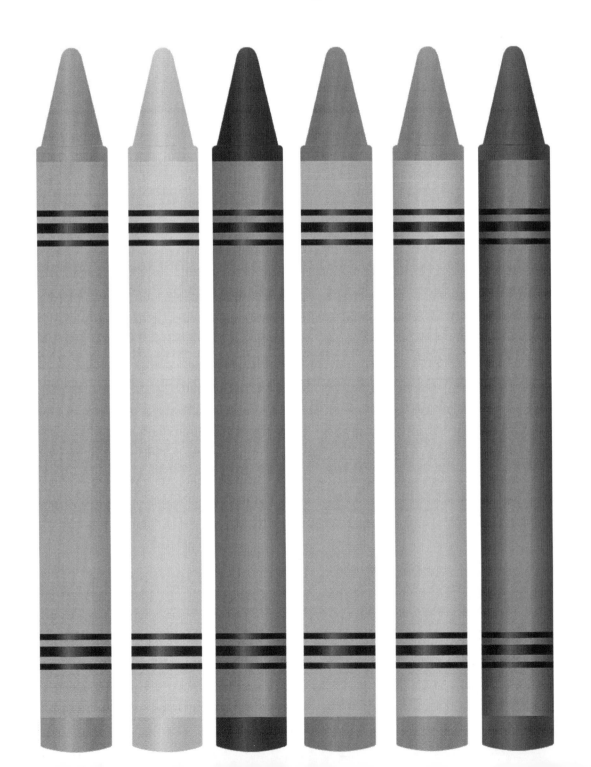

Let's Write!

Use the next few pages
to write some stories.
I know you have a lot to say, and
I can't wait to read it!

Draw a picture for your story!

Draw a picture and write about it on the lines below.

Draw a picture and write about it on the lines below.

Draw a picture and write about it on the lines below.

Draw a picture and write about it on the lines below.

Draw a picture and write about it on the lines below.

Write a story and draw a picture.

Write a story and draw a picture.

Write a story and draw a picture.

Write a story and draw a picture.

It's Maze Time Again!

You're going to need your pencil.

Start

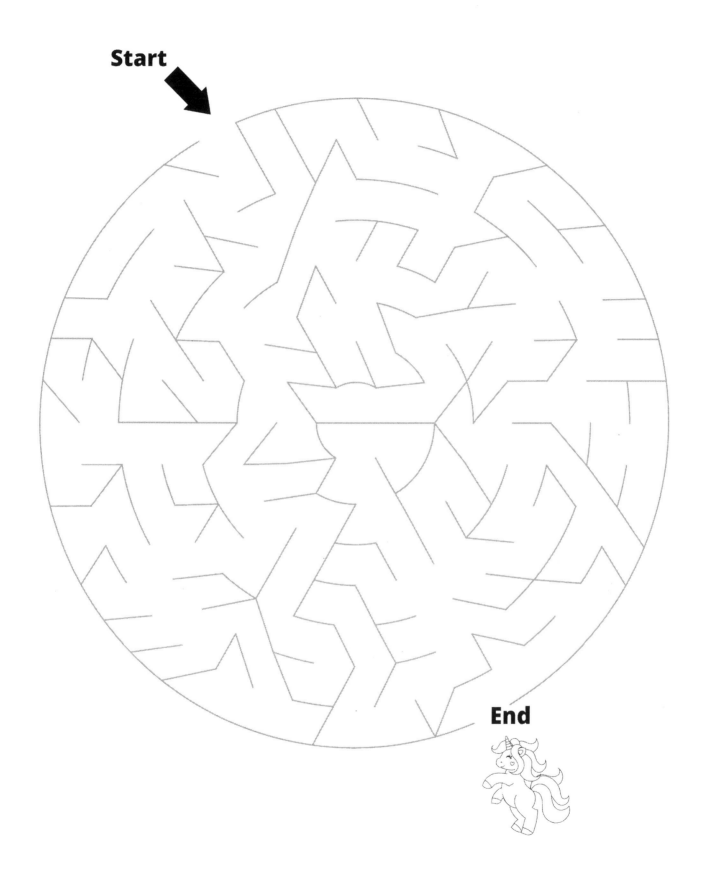

End

Let's check out the answer on the next page.

Start

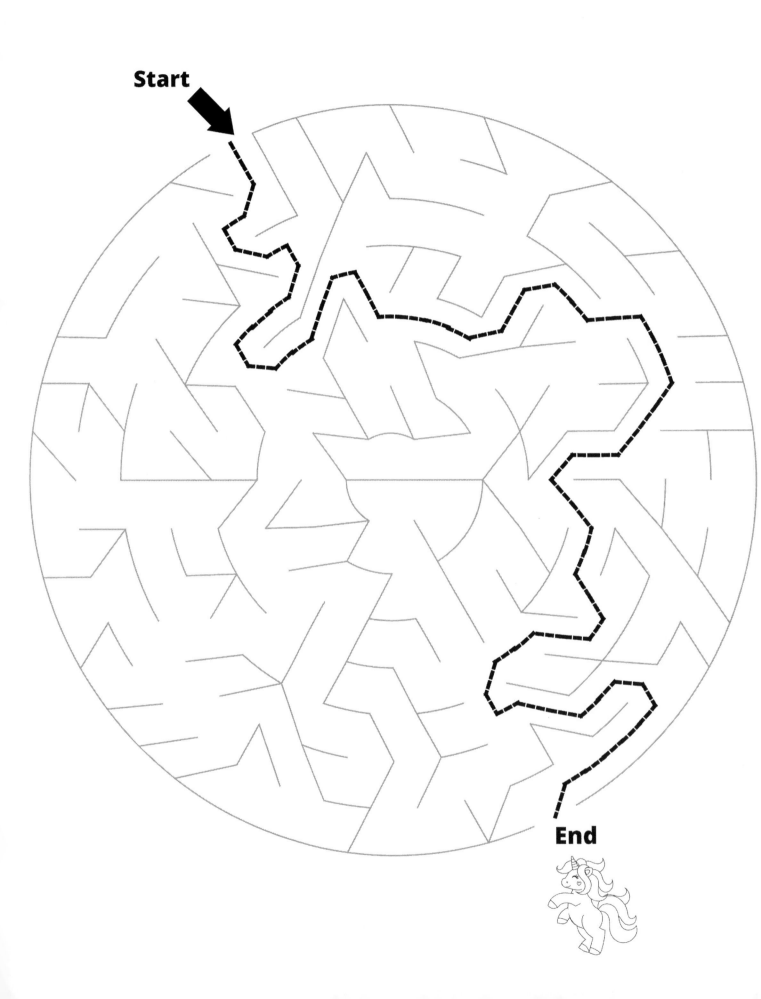

End

Start

End

Let's check out the answer on the next page.

Start

End

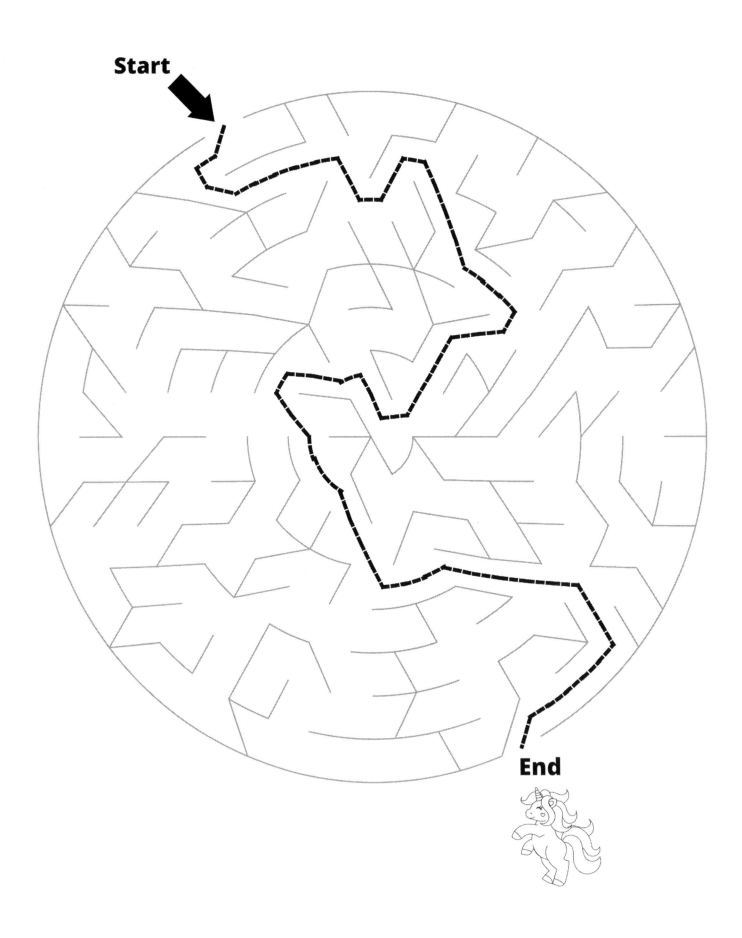

Start

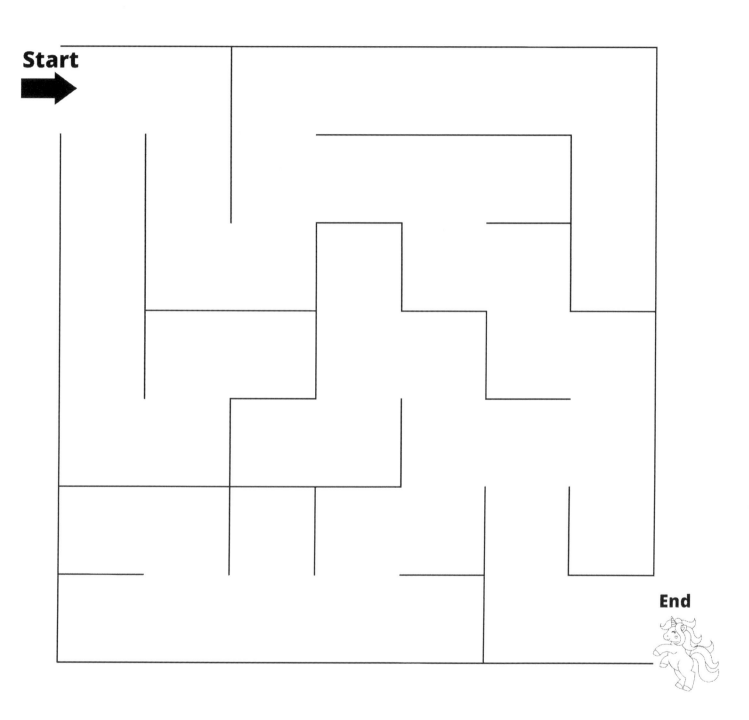

End

Let's check out the answer on the next page.

Start

End

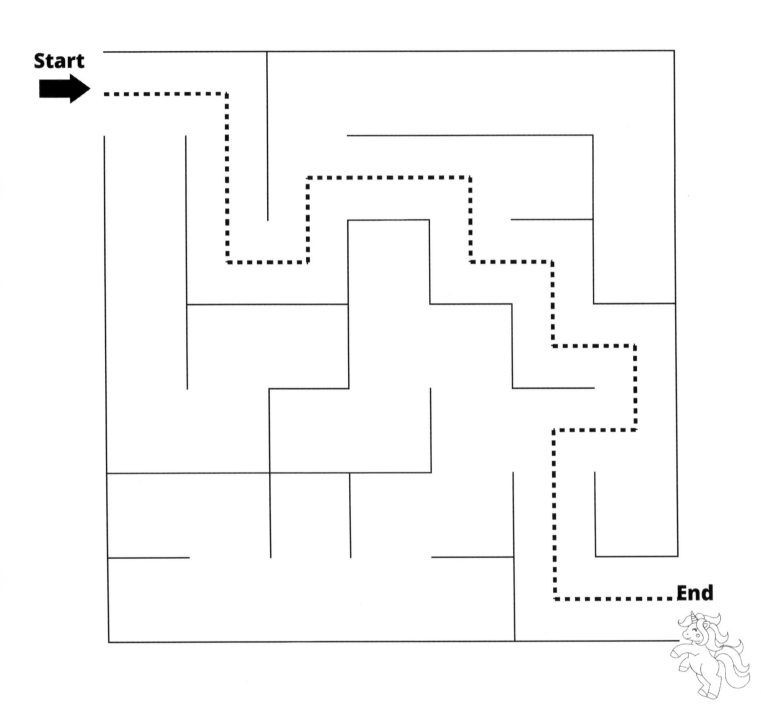

Start

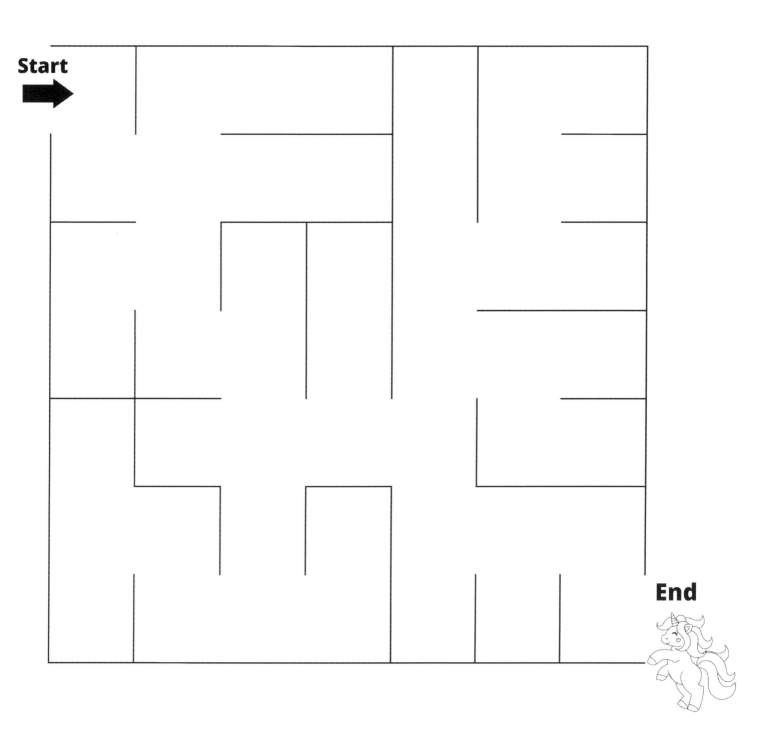

End

Let's check out the answer on the next page.

Start

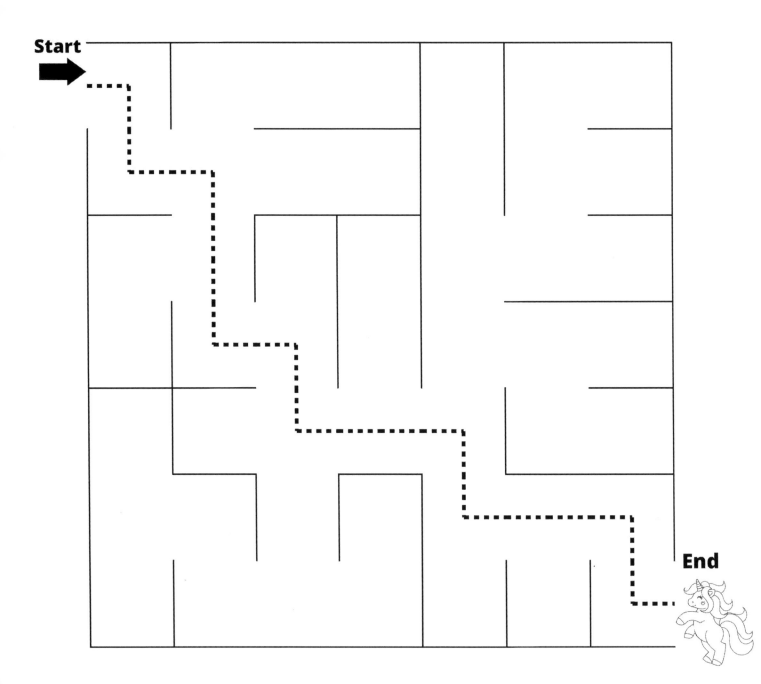

End

Start

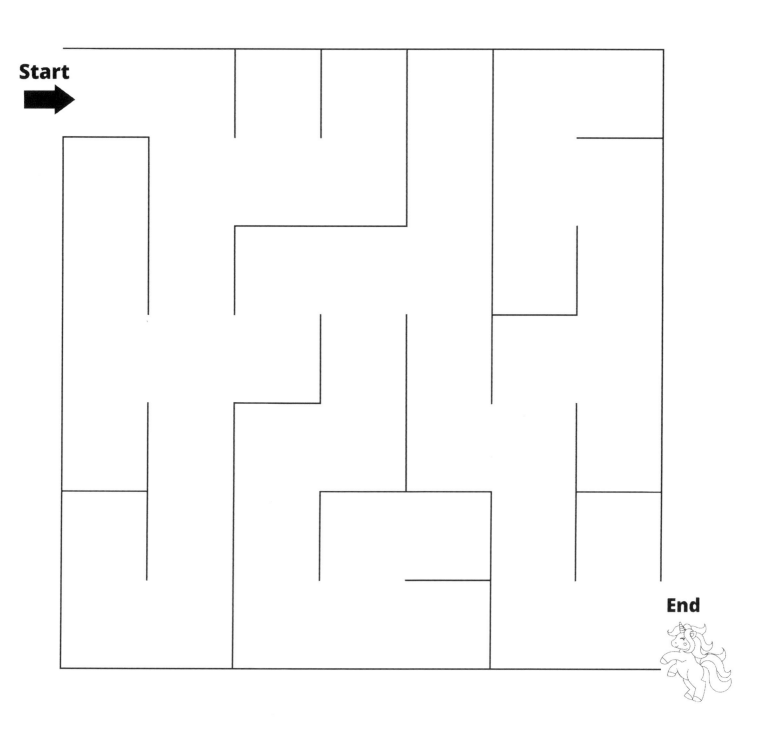

End

Let's check out the answer on the next page.

Start

End

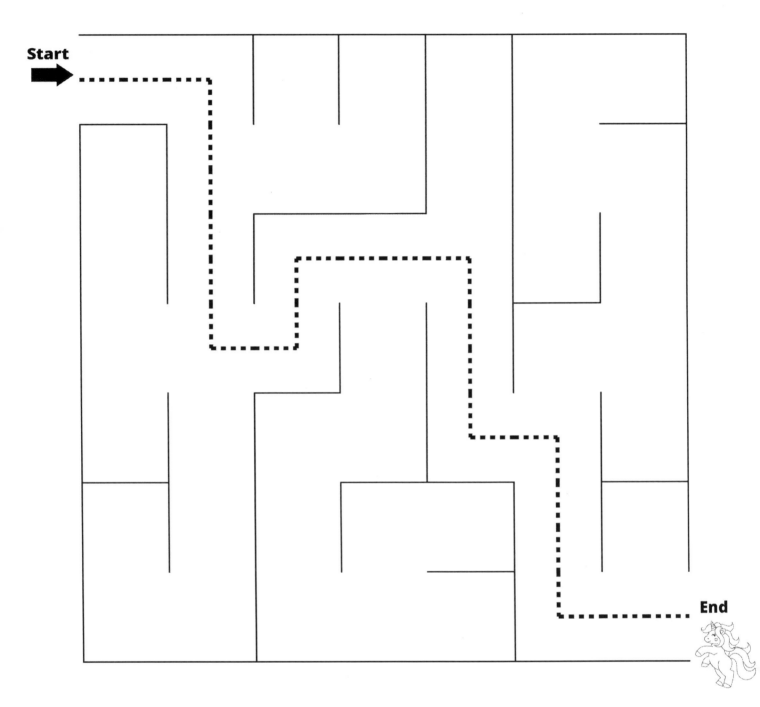

Start

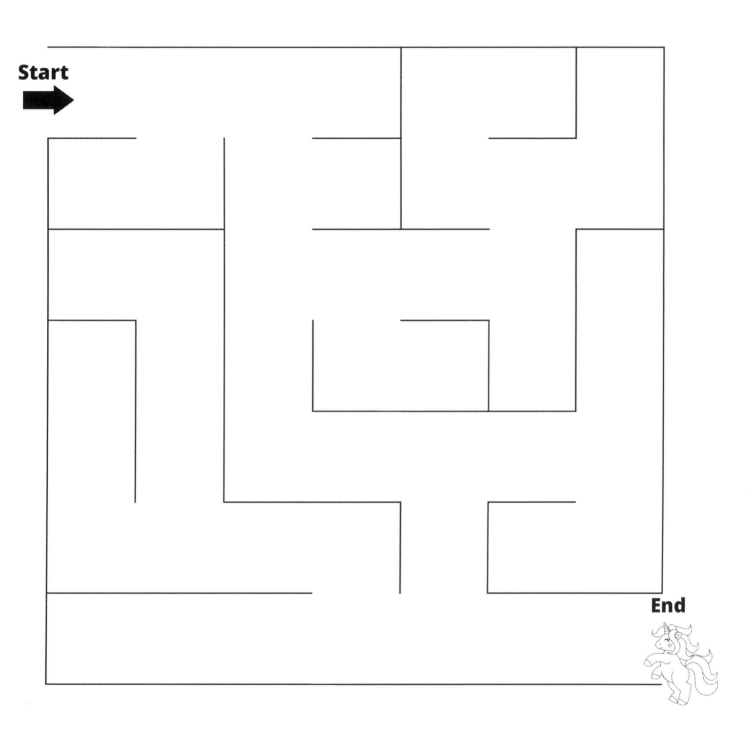

End

Let's check out the answer on the next page.

Start

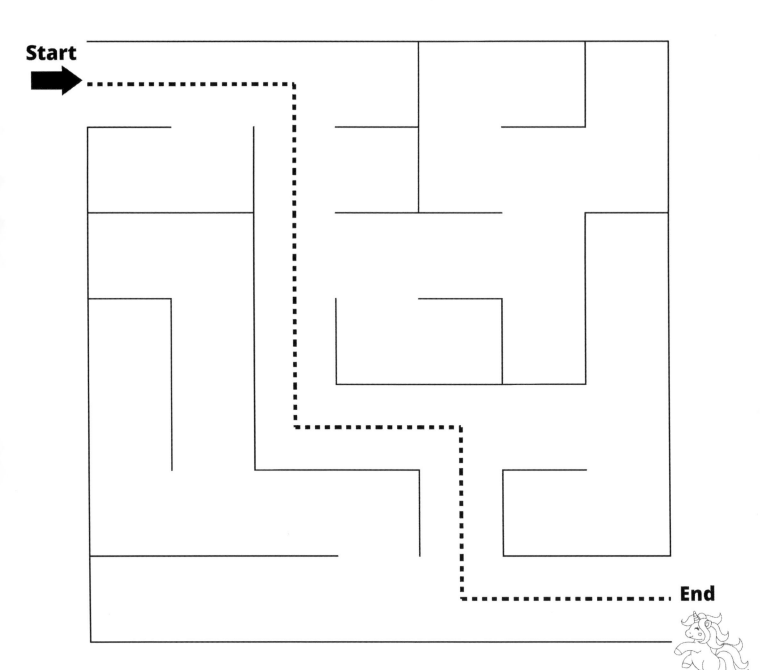

End

Start

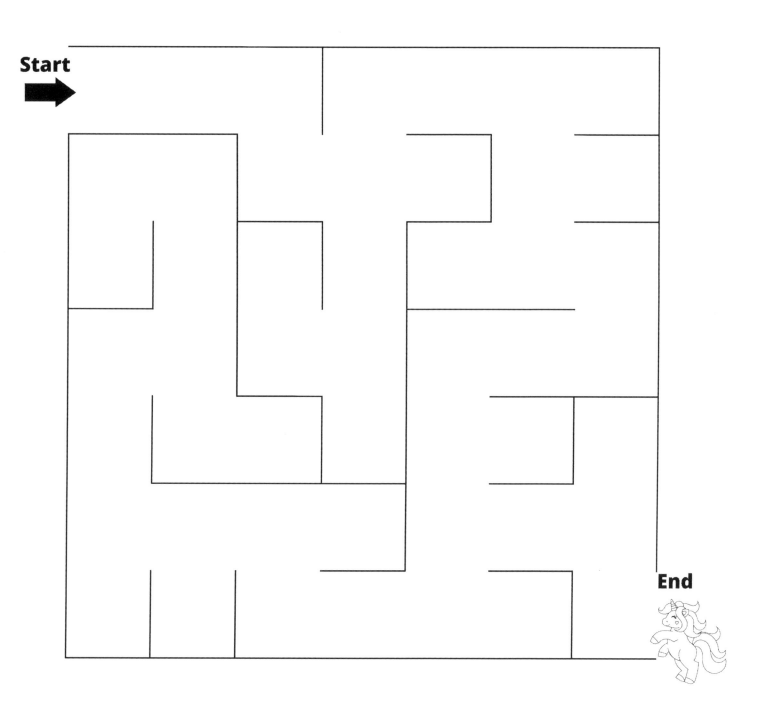

End

Let's check out the answer on the next page.

Start

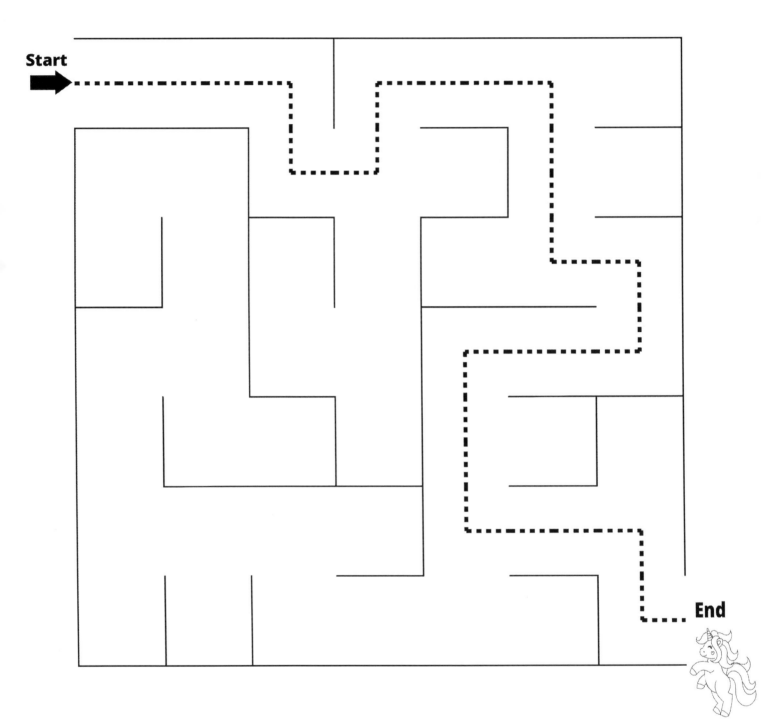

End

It's Crossword Puzzle Time!

Ask someone close to you for help with this puzzle, if needed, but I believe in you! You can do it!

Across
1. The name of your new friend you met in this book.
4. It has wheels and you put it on your foot.
3. You read this.
5. What Uni wanted to grow.

Down
2. What is Uni?
3. This place has water and sand.

Let's check out the answers on the next page.

Across
1. The name of your new friend you met in this book.
4. It has wheels and you put it on your foot.
3. You read this.
5. What Uni wanted to grow.

Down
2. What is Uni?
3. This place has water and sand.

Across
1. Uni ate this at the table.
4. This was one of Uni's favorite things to eat. It's cold.
6. Blue with clouds above your head

Down
2. Uni had many of these.
3. Uni's friend Butter was one of these.
5. Sometimes Uni laid here to talk to Butter.

Let's check out the answers on the next page.

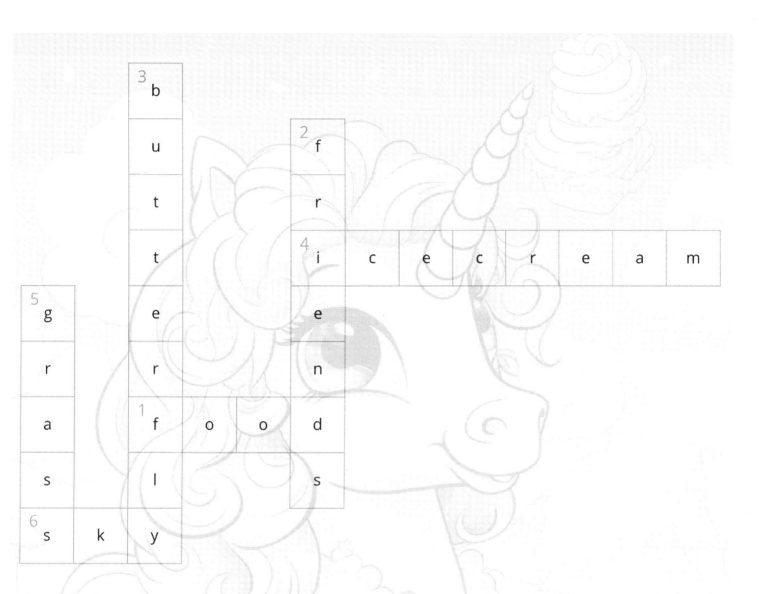

Across
1. Uni ate this at the table.
4. This was one of Uni's favorite things to eat. It's cold.
6. Blue with clouds above your head

Down
2. Uni had many of these.
3. Uni's friend Butter was one of these.
5. Sometimes Uni laid here to talk to Butter.

It's Word Search Time!

Ask someone close to you for help with this puzzle, if needed, but I believe in you! You can do it!

K	U	C	V	N	U	M	S	H	K	R	K
T	N	J	V	B	O	O	K	E	F	E	P
W	I	U	C	I	B	E	A	C	H	Z	I
F	C	N	V	I	U	J	T	I	I	K	Z
R	O	I	U	F	C	A	E	T	U	O	J
W	R	T	Q	F	W	N	N	D	P	G	Y
F	N	S	B	U	V	P	O	N	A	W	Q
T	S	R	D	J	S	S	A	W	G	N	D
Y	L	H	W	Z	O	U	J	U	R	L	A
R	X	V	Z	Q	X	V	X	N	Y	P	B
H	Z	S	K	K	Q	N	O	G	N	O	O
B	C	M	Q	N	U	S	G	F	E	Q	J

Uni   Book   Beach
Skate   Unicorn

Let's check out the answers on the next page.

K	U	C	V	N	U	M	S	H	K	R	K
T	N	J	V	B	O	O	K	E	F	E	P
W	I	U	C	I	B	E	A	C	H	Z	I
F	C	N	V	I	U	J	T	I	I	K	Z
R	O	I	U	F	C	A	E	T	U	O	J
W	R	T	Q	F	W	N	N	D	P	G	Y
F	N	S	B	U	V	P	O	N	A	W	Q
T	S	R	D	J	S	S	A	W	G	N	D
Y	L	H	W	Z	O	U	J	U	R	L	A
R	X	V	Z	Q	X	V	X	N	Y	P	B
H	Z	S	K	K	Q	N	O	G	N	O	O
B	C	M	Q	N	U	S	G	F	E	Q	J

Uni

Skate

Book

Unicorn

Beach

```
B U T T E R F L Y S U I I S
S J T M O N P P F J F H N T G
P Y L K V O E B I N U C H L L
N X X S F N E O P X G M W E
L I P I O X F R L B I W K K
P F F C M W O N U N N K B D
B W R E S H O R N N L M B X
E V I C Z Y D B C P P O I A
F I E R S M X J U T Y A A X
Z R N E J Z O Z Y K J I U L
F N D A U Z L F H O M F S P
H M S M I B W V B W A H R R
J V T O S T P Z K H V U S E
A G T R F Q N Y B X X Y W S
```

Horn   Food   Friends

Butterfly   Ice Cream

Let's check out the answers on the next page.

B	U	T	T	E	R	F	L	Y	S	U	I	I	S
S	J	T	M	O	N	P	F	J	F	H	N	T	G
P	Y	L	K	V	O	E	B	I	N	U	C	H	L
N	X	X	S	F	N	E	O	P	X	G	M	W	E
L	I	P	I	O	X	F	R	L	B	I	W	K	K
P	F	F	C	M	W	O	N	U	N	N	K	B	D
B	W	R	E	S	H	O	R	N	N	L	M	B	X
E	V	I	C	Z	Y	D	B	C	P	P	O	I	A
F	I	E	R	S	M	X	J	U	T	Y	A	A	X
Z	R	N	E	J	Z	O	Z	Y	K	J	I	U	L
F	N	D	A	U	Z	L	F	H	O	M	F	S	P
H	M	S	M	I	B	W	V	B	W	A	H	R	R
J	V	T	O	S	T	P	Z	K	H	V	U	S	E
A	G	T	R	F	Q	N	Y	B	X	X	X	Y	W	S

Horn
Butterfly

Food
Ice Cream

Friends

```
Q   A   G   P   U   W   Z   C   O   K

K   O   M   T   Y   D   H   P   Z   O

F   M   M   O   M   K   S   K   H   P

A   S   V   E   O   F   A   H   A   R

U   S   K   Y   C   L   D   U   P   Y

B   M   G   J   B   H   R   P   P   S

C   Y   Q   R   E   O   U   S   Y   D

S   T   S   B   D   Z   I   J   Q   M

V   S   S   N   I   T   X   N   Y   M

A   G   R   A   S   S   S   F   M   Y
```

Sky   Sad   Mom
Grass   Happy

Let's check out the answers on the next page.

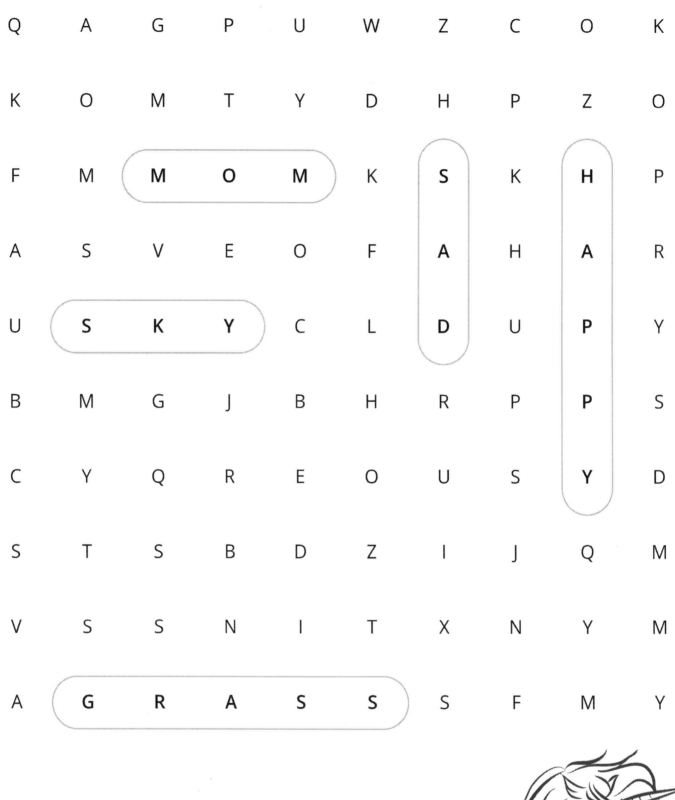

Q	A	G	P	U	W	Z	C	O	K
K	O	M	T	Y	D	H	P	Z	O
F	M	**M**	**O**	**M**	K	**S**	K	**H**	P
A	S	V	E	O	F	**A**	H	**A**	R
U	**S**	**K**	**Y**	C	L	**D**	U	**P**	Y
B	M	G	J	B	H	R	P	**P**	S
C	Y	Q	R	E	O	U	S	**Y**	D
S	T	S	B	D	Z	I	J	Q	M
V	S	S	N	I	T	X	N	Y	M
A	**G**	**R**	**A**	**S**	**S**	S	F	M	Y

Sky   Sad   Mom
Grass   Happy

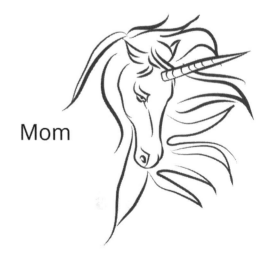

Start

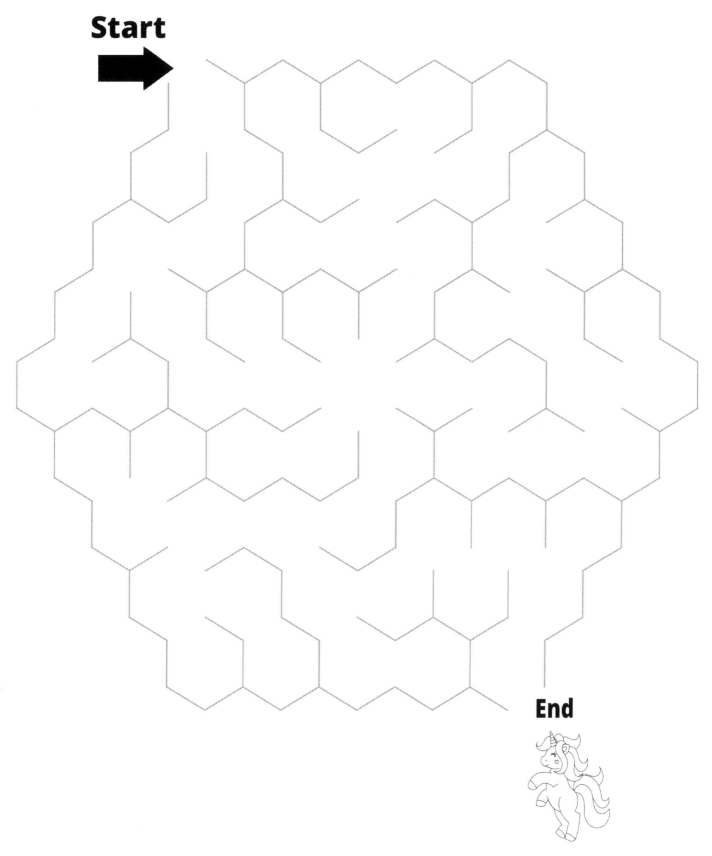

End

Let's check out the answer on the next page.

Start

End

I am so happy to have you as my friend! Maybe one day we can meet at the beach. Until that time, keep reading, writing, drawing and being happy. You are absolutely amazing! There is no one else in the whole world like you!

Made in the USA
Columbia, SC
29 September 2024